For Stella, Olivia, and Fiona
—JV

For A and S
—PZ

Library of Congress Cataloging-in-Publication Data:

Names: Veissid, Jacqueline, author. | Zakimi, Paola, illustrator.
Title: Ruby's sword / by Jacqueline Veissid ; illustrated by Paola Zakimi.
Description: San Francisco, California : Chronicle Books LLC, [2019] | Summary: Ruby wants to play
with her older brothers, but they always ignore her and leave her out of their games—but when Ruby
starts to build her own castle she discovers a way to make her brothers want to play with her.
Identifiers: LCCN 2018027477 | ISBN 9781452163918 (alk. paper)
Subjects: LCSH: Brothers and sisters—Juvenile fiction. | Play—Juvenile fiction. |
Imagination—Juvenile fiction. CYAC: Brothers and sisters—Fiction. | Play—Fiction. | Imagination—Fiction.
Classification: LCC PZ7.1.V442 Ru 2019 | DDC [E]—dc23 LC record available at
https://lccn.loc.gov/2018027477

Manufactured in China.

Design by Sara Gillingham Studio.

Typeset in Nouveau Crayon and Serious Sans.

The illustrations in this book were rendered in watercolor, pencils, and digitally.

10 9 8 7 6 5 4 3 2 1

Chronicle Books LLC
680 Second Street
San Francisco, California 94107

Chronicle Books—we see things differently.
Become part of our community at www.chroniclekids.com.

RUBY'S SWORD

By JACQUELINE VÉISSID

Illustrated by
PAOLA ZAKIMI

chronicle books · san francisco

Ruby raced through a sea of summer grass
after her brothers,
their long legs leaping ahead.

"Wait up!" she called out.

But only their laughter
trailed behind,
like the tail of a kite

just
out
of
reach.

Ruby flopped onto the ground,
heart thumping.

A single cloud sailed across an
endless blue sky.

A warm wind rippled
through the grass,
bending blades . . .

and revealing something hidden.

Swords!

Leaping and lunging.

Swirling and swishing.

Ruby felt invincible.

She raised her sword and
faced the fearsome dragon.
Swish Swish
The dragon faded into a haze.

Ruby gathered the other swords
and marched off.

"I found dragon-fighting swords!" she announced,
slicing the air with lightning bolts.

Her brothers jumped down
to take a closer look.

Ruby granted them
each a sword.

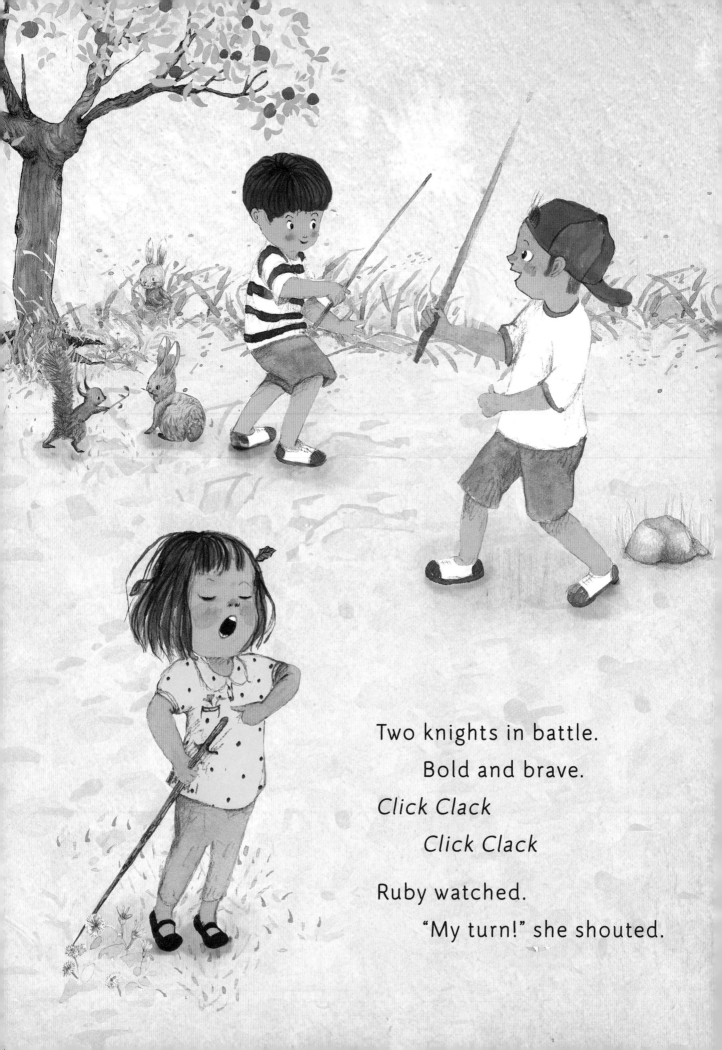

Two knights in battle.

Bold and brave.

Click Clack

Click Clack

Ruby watched.

"My turn!" she shouted.

Click Clack

Click Clack

was all she heard.

Ruby stormed off in a cloud
of dust and disappointment.

The apples hung sky-high.
A royal feast.

The ants were stuck creek side.
Loyal subjects saved.

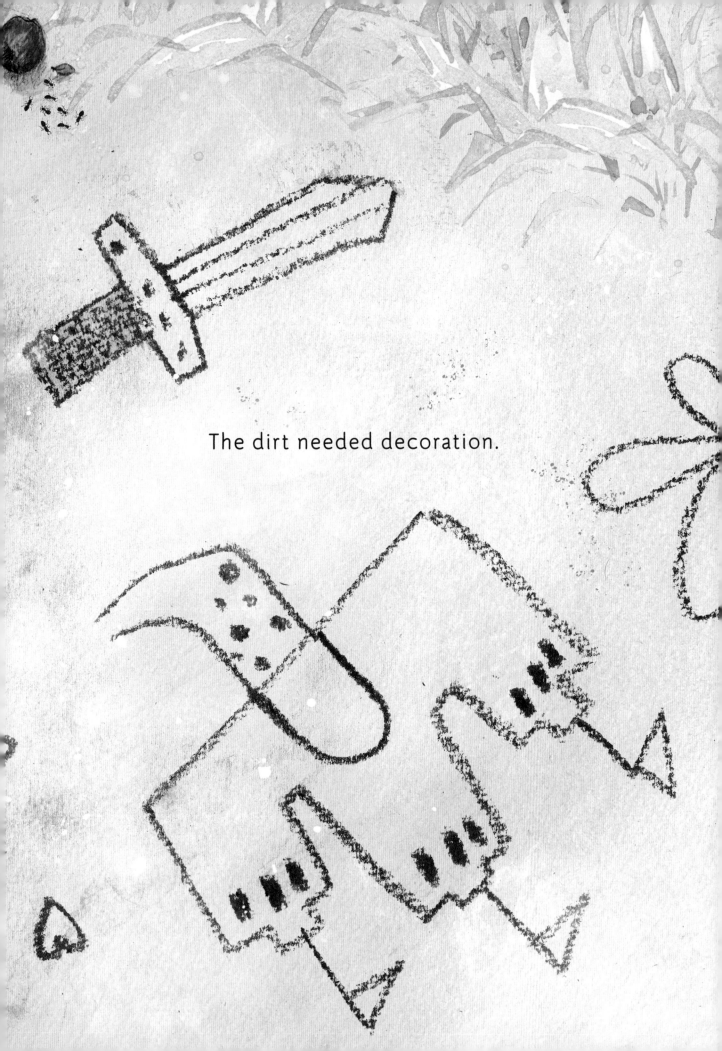

The dirt needed decoration.

A sudden stillness
    filled the air.
Swallows scattered.
    Shadows faded.
A rolling storm
    blanketed the sun.

Ruby raised her trusty sword.

Wild winds
whipped.
Swish Swish

Rumbling clouds
grumbled.
Swish Swish

Raindrops
drummed.
Swish Swish

Ruby gathered
all her strength.
SWISH SWISH!

A mighty gust of wind blew a sheet off a laundry line.

Ruby caught it with her sword.

She began to build.
Click Clack

Her brothers were curious.
"Can we help?" they asked.

Click Clack
was all they heard.

They marched away . . .

and returned with some honorable offerings.

Twigs.

Rocks.

A handful of dandelions.

And finally,
their swords.

Together they built a magnificent castle.

Click Clack

Click Clack

Click Clack

Perfect for sheltering many loyal subjects.

And three noble knights.